For Max, my own little happy – L.B.
My gift to you, Fiana – A.R.

HODDER CHILDREN'S BOOKS

First published in Great Britain in 2019 by Hodder and Stoughton

Text © Laura Baker 2019
Illustrations © Angie Rozelaar 2019

A CIP catalogue record for this book
is available from the British Library.

HB ISBN: 978 1 444 93967 5
PB ISBN: 978 1 444 93968 2

1 3 5 7 9 10 8 6 4 2

Printed and bound in China.

Hodder Children's Books
An imprint of
Hachette Children's Group
Part of Hodder and Stoughton
Carmelite House
50 Victoria Embankment
London, EC4Y 0DZ

An Hachette UK Company
www.hachette.co.uk

www.hachettechildrens.co.uk

the COLOUR of HAPPY

Laura Baker
Angie Rozelaar

Hodder
Children's
Books

Blue is for the calm I feel wandering in the spring.

Yellow
is for happy
when I spot
a special
thing.

Skip and hop and skip and hop,

and run and jump and play.

Dark blue is for sadness
when my treasure blows **a w a y . . .**

Red is for my anger

when I have to

watch it go.

Green is for my envy when

someone has what's MINE.

I'm feeling **grey**

and don't believe
that it will all be fine.

A kind friend, a thankful nod,

but watch it float and

soar!

Gold is for the hope I feel chasing it once more.

Skip and hop
and share
and hop,

and run and play
and then . . .

Purple is for proud
when at last it's mine again.

Orange is for excitement that
I feel through and through . . .

And **pink** is for the love
I have, giving my gift to you.